Katie Kazoo, SWITCHEROO

Holly's Jolly Christmas

ISBN: 978-0-545-20932-8

12 11 10 9 8 7 6 5 4   10 11 12 13 14/0

Printed in the U.S.A.   40

First Scholastic printing, December 2009

For Connie, Glenn, Mally, and Tess. Thanks for all the holly, jolly Christmases.—NK

For those elves from the Great White North: Eric and Kelly—J&W

Katie Kazoo, SWITCHEROO

Holly's Jolly Christmas

by Nancy Krulik • illustrated by John & Wendy

SCHOLASTIC INC.
New York Toronto London Auckland
Sydney Mexico City New Delhi Hong Kong

Chapter 1

Sally, Cathy, Luis, and Chuck each have their own Christmas tree. Each tree has a different number of candy canes, and a different number of decorations. Use the clues to figure out . . .

Katie Carew tried really hard to focus on her math worksheet. But it was so difficult. Not the math—actually, Katie was pretty good at doing these kinds of puzzles. It was just really, *really* hard to think about schoolwork when Christmas was so near!

Growl. Grumble.

Just then, Katie heard a really strange noise coming from the beanbag next to her.

"Sorry," George Brennan apologized. "That

was my stomach. Reading about candy canes is making me hungry."

Katie giggled. It didn't take much to make George hungry.

"I know what you mean," George's best friend, Kevin Camilleri, agreed. "I can't stop thinking about the tomato and mozzarella salad my grandmother makes every Christmas Eve."

"It seems like you dudes are already on your holiday break," Mr. Guthrie told the class. But he didn't seem angry. Mr. G. *never* got angry.

"It's just that Christmas is only a week away," Katie explained to her teacher.

"I'm so excited, I can't sit still," George added.

"You *never* sit still," Kadeem Carter told George.

George laughed. "That's true."

"Well, George," Mr. G. said. "If you can't sit still, stand up."

"What?" George asked.

The kids watched as Mr. G. went to the closet in the back of the room. He pulled out a huge bag of blown-up balloons. He was also holding a pair of red long underwear.

"Here, George," Mr. G. said, handing him the long underwear. "Put this on over your clothes."

George looked at their teacher strangely. Katie knew why. Putting on long underwear was a really strange request—even from Mr. G. And Mr. G. made *a lot* of strange requests.

But George did what he was told.

"Now, while George is putting on the long underwear, I'm going to divide the rest of you into teams," Mr. G. said. "Katie, Emma W., and Andy, you'll be Team One."

Katie grinned. Emma Weber was her closest friend in class 4A. And Andy Epstein was the best athlete. So she was on a great team—no matter what weird game they were going to play. And considering the game included balloons and underwear, it was sure to be weird.

Once Mr. G. had put the kids into groups, he explained the game. "For this game, George is Santa."

"George doesn't look anything like Santa," Mandy Banks said. "He doesn't have whiskers or a big belly."

Mr. G. smiled. "Not yet!" Then he pulled a white, cotton beard out of his desk drawer. "Here, George."

George put on the beard. Katie giggled. George looked really silly.

"I gave Santa his whiskers," Mr. G. told the kids. "Now you are going to give him his belly."

Huh? The kids all stared at Mr. G. Now they were *very* confused.

"Each team will have twenty seconds to fill Santa's long underwear with balloons," Mr. G. explained. "The team who puts the most balloons into Santa's underwear will win. Team One, you're up first."

Katie, Andy, and Emma W. were given a bunch of green balloons.

"Okay, Team One," Mr. G. said. "On your marks. Get set. Go!"

Katie worked as fast as she could, picking up

balloons and shoving them into George's long red underwear. It was hard. Especially because George kept squirming around.

"Hey! That tickles, Katie Kazoo!" George shouted as Katie shoved in a green balloon.

Katie grinned. She loved when George called her by the way-cool nickname he had given her back in third grade.

Bam! Hisssss!

Suddenly, a funny sound started coming from George's behind.

"What was that?" Kevin asked.

"One of the balloons popped," George said.

In the end, Team Three won. They managed to stuff five balloons into George's long underwear, although three popped.

"That game was hilarious," Santa George said, laughing.

Katie giggled, too. The game *was* hilarious! But that was no surprise. There was always something funny, or exciting, or interesting going on in Mr. G.'s classroom.

The way Katie figured, being in class 4A was like getting a Christmas present every day. You never knew what you were going to find inside. But whatever it was, you were sure to like it!

Chapter 2

Katie smiled happily as she unpacked her lunch in the school cafeteria later that day. Her lettuce, tomato, and cheese sandwich had been cut in the shape of a Christmas tree. And she had a red and white candy cane for dessert. Her mom was so nice.

"This is almost too pretty to eat," Katie said, staring at the sandwich.

"I've lost my appetite," Katie's best friend, Suzanne Lock, said. She pointed across the table at George's food tray. "Why do you do that?" she asked him.

George had mixed his mashed potatoes, green beans, and milk into a big, gray-green,

mushy soup. "It's fun," George answered.

"It's fun to smush your food together?"

"It's fun to bug you," George explained to Suzanne. He shot her a huge smile.

Suzanne rolled her eyes. "You don't bug me, George. I have much bigger problems than your lunch."

"What's wrong, Suzanne?" Katie asked.

Katie's other best friend, Jeremy Fox, rolled his eyes. "Oh no," he moaned. "Here we go."

Katie sighed. It made her crazy that her friends didn't like each other.

But if Suzanne had heard Jeremy's comment, she didn't act like it. Instead, she frowned and said, "My sister is what's wrong."

Katie looked at Suzanne strangely. "Heather's not even two years old. What did she do?"

"It's what my mother did *with* Heather," Suzanne explained. "She thought it would be fun for Heather to be in the holiday show down at the Community Center. It's a play about these broken toys who want to be given to children for Christmas. Heather's going to be the baby doll."

"Aww. That sounds so cute," Katie said.

Suzanne shot Katie an angry look. "Whose side are you on?" she demanded.

"Yours," Katie assured her. "I just think Heather kind of looks like a baby doll."

"Yeah, well, she's a *baby,* anyway," Suzanne said. "All she has to do is sit in the sleigh and say 'Mama, Mama' over and over again."

"I still don't understand what *your* problem is," Jeremy said.

"You don't understand anything," Suzanne groaned. "Everyone is making such a big fuss over Heather. I don't know why it's such a big deal. She's not even acting. 'Mama' is one of the only words she can say. And she's only on stage for a minute."

Now Katie understood why Suzanne was so upset. She hated it when anyone else was the center of attention.

"My contribution to the show is much more important," Suzanne continued.

"You're in the show, too?" George asked her.

"Not in it," Suzanne said. "I'm in *charge* of it. I'm the stage manager. Well, actually I'm the student stage manager. There's a grown-up stage manager, too. But it's the same thing."

"What exactly does a stage manager do?" Jeremy asked her.

"I can't believe you don't know," Suzanne told him.

"I don't, either," Katie admitted.

"Oh," Suzanne said, sounding a lot nicer than she did when she was talking to Jeremy. "A stage manager is the person who makes sure all the scenery is in the right place, and that all the actors are in their costumes and ready to go onstage when they're supposed to. A stage manager runs things."

"So basically you just boss people around," Jeremy said. "That's the perfect job for you."

George began to laugh.

Suzanne shot the boys a dirty look. Then she turned to Katie. "We need someone to help paint scenery," she told her. "You did a really great job for our school play. Could you do it for the Community Center play, too?"

"I don't know, Suzanne," Katie started. "I have a lot of things . . ."

"Oh, come on, Katie," Suzanne urged. "Where's your Christmas spirit?"

Katie sighed. She knew Suzanne wasn't going to give up until she got what she wanted. She never did. So she figured she might as well spare them both the time and energy.

"Okay, I'll help," she said.

"Great!" Suzanne high-fived Katie. "The story takes place in a magical Christmas forest. So you have to paint lots of Christmas trees. You'll love it."

"It does sort of sound like fun," Katie admitted.

Suzanne smiled at her. "It *will* be fun. I'm going to be a great stage manager. The best ever. By the time I get finished with this show, everyone will be talking about me."

Katie rolled her eyes. That was exactly what she was afraid of. Whenever Suzanne became the center of attention, trouble was sure to follow.

Chapter 3

Katie wasn't thinking about Suzanne or the Community Center show as she walked home that afternoon. She was thinking about Christmas again. It was hard not to. Even before she turned the corner onto her block, she could hear Christmas carols.

"We wish you a merry Christmas. We wish you a merry Christmas. We wish you a merry Christmas, and a happy New Year."

The music wasn't coming from real live singers. It was blasting from the huge speakers on the roof of Mr. Brigandi's house.

By now, Katie was used to hearing the song. It had been playing over and over for a week now—ever since Mr. Brigandi had put up his Christmas decorations. The song was the background music for the twirling Sugar Plum Fairy and marching Nutcracker on her neighbor's front lawn.

"Ho, ho, ho!"

As Katie walked further down the block, she heard Santa's loud, jolly laughter coming from Mrs. Derkman's house. Mrs. Derkman and her husband loved decorating their house for Christmas every bit as much as Mr. Brigandi did.

This year, the Derkmans had placed a huge, rubbery Santa Claus on their front lawn. The Santa sat in a sleigh that moved back and forth on a track. As the sleigh moved, the Santa shouted "Ho, ho, ho" over and over.

Katie's house was decorated for Christmas, too. It looked pretty with its colorful flashing lights and electric candles in the windows. But it was nothing compared to what her neighbors had done.

"Ruff! Ruff! Ruff!"

Just then, Katie's chocolate and white cocker spaniel, Pepper, came bounding out of the house to greet her.

"Arf! Arf! Arf!"

Pepper's best friend, Snowball, was right behind him.

Katie giggled as the two dogs jumped up and down, rubbing their fuzzy bodies against her legs. They looked so cute.

"I love your new coat," Katie told Pepper. Her dog was wearing a green and red plaid doggie jacket.

Pepper wagged his stubby, little tail happily. He didn't know exactly what Katie had said, but he could tell it was something nice.

"And your hat is really cute, Snowball," Katie added. "I love the antlers."

Snowball barked and wagged her tail at the sound of her name.

As Katie bent down to pet Pepper and Snowball, she noticed two motorcycles parked in the driveway. She broke out into a huge smile.

"Grandma and Nick are here!" Katie exclaimed. She jumped up and ran toward the door.

"Well, hello there!" Katie's grandmother said, as Katie raced into the living room.

"Hi, Grandma!" Katie exclaimed. She gave her grandmother a big hug.

"What? No hugs for me?" Nick asked.

Katie reached over and wrapped her arms around Nick. It wasn't easy. Nick had kind of a big belly.

"Wow, your beard got so long," Katie told Nick.

"I combed it out really nice just for you," Nick said, stroking his long, white beard.

"It seems like you grew a foot since I last saw you," Katie's grandmother told her.

Katie stood up straight so she would look even taller. Then she sniffed at the air. "Mmmm, it smells so Christmas-y in here."

"We've been baking gingerbread," Nick told her. "I know it's your favorite."

"It was your mother's favorite, too, when she was your age," Katie's grandmother told her.

Katie looked around. "Where *is* mom?"

"At work," Nick said. "Things are really busy now."

Katie knew that was true. Her mom was the manager of the Book Nook bookstore in the Cherrydale Mall. At Christmastime, she was also the store's chief gift wrapper.

Thinking about that gave Katie a great idea. "If Mom and Dad aren't home, then this is the perfect time to wrap their gifts."

"It sure is," Nick told her.

"I'm going to put lots of ribbons and stickers on the packages, so they look really pretty under the tree," Katie said. Then she sighed. "If we ever get a tree. Mom and Dad have been too busy to buy one."

"I did notice something was missing around here," Nick said.

As far as Katie was concerned, Christmas

just wasn't Christmas without a big tree in the living room.

"I wi . . ." Katie began. Then she stopped herself.

Phew. That had been close. She'd almost wished for a tree. But Katie never made wishes. *Ever*.

Chapter 4

It had all started back in third grade on one terrible, horrible, miserable day. First, Katie had missed the football and lost the game for her team. Then she'd fallen in the mud and ruined her brand-new, favorite jeans. And then she'd stood up in front of the whole class, and let out the biggest, loudest burp in the history of Cherrydale Elementary School. Talk about embarrassing.

That night, Katie had wished that she could be anyone but herself. There must have been a shooting star overhead or something, because the next day the magic wind arrived.

The magic wind was a wild, powerful

tornado that blew only around Katie. The magic wind was so strong that it was able to blow her right out of her own body into someone else's. One . . . two . . . switcheroo!

The first time the magic wind came, it turned her into Speedy the class hamster. Katie had spent the whole morning stuck in a cage, going around and around on a hamster wheel and eating wooden chew sticks. When she finally escaped from the cage, she wound up in George's stinky gym sneaker! Boy was Katie happy when the magic wind returned and blew her back into herself again!

The trouble was Katie never stayed herself for long. The magic wind came back again and again. Once it turned her into Lucille, the lunch lady. Katie started a food fight with gooey egg salad and almost got the real Lucille fired.

Another time, the magic wind turned Katie into Mike Reed, the shortstop for the Cherrydale Porcupines. Mike was an amazing baseball player. Unfortunately, Katie wasn't. She struck out, and dropped an important fly ball. Then she started to cry—and everyone in the stadium saw her on the jumbotron screen. Only they thought it was Mike who was sobbing. The poor guy!

And then there was the time the magic wind switcherooed Katie into Slinky, class 4A's pet snake. Just thinking about shedding Slinky's skin still made her itch. Most fourth-grade girls don't shed.

The magic wind was the reason Katie didn't make wishes anymore. She knew what kinds of weird things could happen if they came true.

But she still really, really wanted a Christmas tree, even if she couldn't wish for one.

Luckily, Katie didn't *have* to wish this time. Instead, Nick said, "I think we should go to a tree farm and pick one out."

"When?" Katie asked him.

"How about right now?" Grandma

suggested. "No time like the present."

"And no present like a Christmas present," Katie giggled.

"Good one," Nick complimented her.

"Won't your mom and dad be surprised when they come home from work!" Katie's grandmother added.

Katie was already at the front door.

"Whoa, hold it right there," Nick said.

Katie stopped in her tracks. "What's wrong? You said we could go now."

"Don't you think you ought to put your coat on first?" Nick asked. "It's as cold as the North Pole out there."

"The perfect weather for buying a Christmas tree," Katie's grandmother said.

Katie grinned. She couldn't have agreed more!

Chapter 5

"We're here! We're here!" Katie shouted excitedly as Nick parked the car outside the tree farm. She was bouncing up and down in her seat like a little kid. But Katie couldn't help it. There was just something about Christmastime that made her *feel* like a little kid again.

"Come on, hurry up," Katie urged as she leaped out of the car and ran toward the trees. "Pllleeease."

"I'm just locking the car," her grandmother called. "You go on ahead. We'll catch up with you." Then she breathed in deeply. "Mmmm . . . smell that pine."

Katie sniffed at the air and smiled brightly.

She loved the smell of pine trees and cold air all mixed together. It was the smell of Christmas, and it was wonderful.

Other people obviously felt the same way. All around her, people were smiling, laughing, and humming Christmas carols as they examined the trees. Everyone at the tree farm seemed to have the Christmas spirit.

Well, almost everyone, anyway. Behind the cash register was a woman wearing a cheerful, red and white Santa hat, and a tree-shaped nametag that said "Holly." Holly was a very jolly name. But this Holly didn't look so jolly.

"Can you tell me where the medium-sized trees are?" Katie overheard one woman ask.

Holly pointed, and said, "Over there."

"But *all* the trees are over there," the woman said.

Holly shrugged. "Yeah, and some of them are medium sized. You'll just have to look through them all to find what you want."

Katie couldn't believe it. How could

someone who worked at a Christmas tree farm not have Christmas spirit? This was the most Christmas-y job there was. Except for Santa's job, of course.

Just then, someone with *lots* of Christmas spirit snuck up behind Katie. "Guess who?" the person asked.

Katie turned around fast. "Louie!" she shouted out happily. Louie owned the pizzeria next to the bookstore in the Cherrydale Mall. Of all the people who worked at the mall, he was her favorite. "What are you doing here?" she asked.

"I'm picking out a tree," Louie said. "What else do you do at a Christmas tree farm?"

Katie giggled. "That's true," she said. "But if you're here, who's at the pizzeria?"

"My wife's in charge today," he told her. "She can keep the customers happy until I get back."

Katie didn't know Louie's wife, but if she was half as nice as Louie she would definitely be able to keep all the customers happy!

"I know your mom's working today, so who are you here with? Your dad?" Louie asked Katie.

"No. My Grandma and her friend, Nick," Katie told him. "But when you get back to the mall, don't tell my mom you saw us. We want the tree to be a surprise."

Louie smiled. "My lips are sealed!"

"I want to find a tree that is big, but not too big," she told Louie. "It has to fit in my living room." She looked around at the trees that were for sale at the farm. "Gee. Most of the trees look kind of small and scrawny."

Suddenly, an angry voice said, "Well, what do you expect?"

Katie swerved around. It was Holly.

Holly's hands were on her hips. "It's a week before Christmas. Most of the really full trees are gone," she said. "You gotta come early if that's what you want, girlie."

Katie turned red. She hadn't meant for Holly to hear what she'd said about the trees.

"I'm sorry," Katie apologized.

Holly frowned. She pointed to the rows and rows of Christmas trees. "That's what's left. Take 'em or leave 'em."

Louie shrugged at Katie as if to say he didn't understand why Holly was so cranky. Then he waved good-bye to Katie.

Katie was not going to let Holly take all the fun out of buying a tree. So she gave Holly the biggest smile she could. "I'm sure I'll find the perfect tree here."

Holly didn't bother to answer. She started to march away.

"Merry Christmas," Katie said.

Holly sighed and rolled her eyes. "Whatever," she said.

Chapter 6

"Oh Christmas tree, oh Christmas tree . . ." Katie hummed as she walked between the rows of pine trees. She could see her grandmother and Nick at the other end of the farm, examining trees. She waved. But they were too far away to see her.

There weren't many big trees. Katie guessed Holly was right. They should have come sooner. Then she turned down another row. Yes! There were a few that were nice and round and full—even if they weren't very tall.

She held out her hand and fingered the pine needles on a cute, little tree. Then she leaned down and took a deep sniff of the tree's sweet piney scent. *Mmmm.*

Katie let out a happy little sigh. It was sooooo nice being here, just her and the Christmas trees. It felt like she was alone in a magical Christmas forest.

"I should try and remember just how these trees look right now," Katie said to herself. That way she could make them look real when she painted the scenery for the Community Center play.

But as Katie continued looking at the trees, she felt a cool breeze blowing on the back of her neck.

Brrrr. She tightened her scarf, and pulled down her ski hat. But the cool breeze didn't go away. In fact, it started to get stronger and stronger.

Katie looked around at the trees. The branches didn't seem to be blowing at all. In fact, they were just standing there, straight and still. But the wind kept moving, blowing harder and harder . . . *and circling just around Katie.*

Katie gulped. That could only mean one thing. This might not be a magical forest, but that breeze was definitely the *magic* wind!

"Oh no!" Katie cried out. "Not now. Not while I'm shopping for my Christmas tree! Go away, magic wind. *Please!*"

But the magic wind didn't listen to Katie. It just kept blowing harder and harder. It was freezing cold, and chilled her to the bone. Katie was afraid that this time the wind could turn her into a block of ice, right there in the middle of the Christmas tree farm.

Or worse, it could blow her far, far away. Maybe all the way to the North Pole!

Katie shut her eyes tight, and tried not to cry.

And then it stopped. Just like that.

The magic wind was gone. And so was

Katie Kazoo.

One, two, switcheroo. Katie was someone new. But who?

Chapter 7

"How much is this wreath, ma'am?" Katie heard a man asking her. The voice was awfully familiar.

Katie opened her eyes slowly and came face to face with Nick. He was holding a large, green wreath in his hands.

"Nick!" Katie exclaimed happily. She was very glad to see that she was still at the tree farm, and that Nick was still there with her.

But Nick looked at her strangely. "Do I know you?" he asked her.

"Of course!" Katie exclaimed. "I'm . . ."

Katie stopped herself in midsentence. She wasn't sure who she was anymore. The magic wind had changed all that.

"I don't think we've ever met," Nick continued. "How did you know my name?"

Katie gulped. How was she supposed to answer that? She couldn't just tell Nick about the magic wind or anything.

"Well . . . um . . . I called you Nick, because, well . . . um . . . you look like Santa Claus," Katie said. "You know, Jolly St. Nick."

"Ho, ho, ho," Nick chuckled. "It must be my white beard."

Katie smiled. "Yeah, that's it."

"Well, I know your name, too," Nick told her.

"You do?" Katie asked. "How?"

"It says it right there on your nametag," Nick said. "It's nice to meet you . . . *Holly*."

Katie gulped. She looked down at her feet. Instead of her pink and white snow boots, she was wearing heavy, black boots. And instead of her pretty, new winter jacket, she was wearing a thick, dark green parka. There was a tree-shaped nametag on the parka. The tag had the name "Holly" written on it.

Katie gasped. Oh no! The magic wind had turned Katie into the very un-jolly Holly!

"I was hoping to buy this wreath as a surprise for a very special fourth-grade girl," Nick told her. "But I'm not sure how much it costs."

Katie smiled. Nick was buying her the wreath as a surprise. Of course, it wasn't a surprise anymore. But Nick didn't know that. And Katie would never tell him.

"Isn't there a price tag on it?" Katie asked.

Nick shook his head. "There was a price on some of the other ones, but not this one," he told her.

"I guess it costs the same as the other ones," Katie said, trying to sound like someone who worked at a tree farm. "How much were they?"

"That one with the silver tinsel is ten dollars," Nick told Katie. "It's smaller, though."

It actually was quite a bit smaller. Katie didn't know what to do. She finally said. "Since

there's no price, I'll just charge you ten dollars for this one, even though it's bigger."

"Well, thanks!" Nick said. He reached into his pocket and pulled out a bill.

Katie went and placed the money in the cash register, just like she'd seen her mom do at the bookstore at the mall.

"Thank you very much," Katie told him.

"I'm going to go put this wreath in the trunk of my car," Nick told her. "If a girl with bright red pigtails comes over, don't tell her I bought her the wreath."

Katie smiled. "I won't. I promise," she assured him.

"Merry Christmas," Nick said as he walked away.

"Merry Christmas," Katie told him.

Just then, a woman in a blue and yellow checked coat walked up to Katie. "I've chosen a tree, and I'd like someone to help me bring it to my car," she said.

"Oh," Katie said. "I don't think I can carry a

tree by myself."

"Don't you have men who work here to help carry the trees?" the woman asked.

"I don't know," Katie said. "I don't see any. Do you?"

The woman looked at her curiously.

Oops. Katie had forgotten she was Holly now. "I mean, let me find someone to help you."

Katie stepped away from behind the counter and started to walk toward the trees.

"Hey, where are you going?" a man in a black coat asked her. "I've been waiting in line to pay for five minutes." He held up a small Christmas tree.

"I'll just be a minute, sir," Katie said, trying to sound polite.

"I'm kind of in a hurry," the man explained. "My office is having a Christmas party this afternoon, and I said I'd bring a tree."

"What a great idea!" Katie exclaimed.

"Excuse me," the woman in the blue and yellow checked coat interrupted. "But I was ahead of him. You were helping me first."

"But I'll only be a minute," the man with the small Christmas tree said. "I can't be late!"

Just then, a woman and a small boy hurried over to the counter. "Do you have a bathroom?" she asked Katie. "Joshie here has just been potty trained, and he really has to go."

Katie looked down. Joshie was moving back and forth on his feet. He did look like he had to go to the bathroom right away. But she didn't see a bathroom anywhere. Not even a porta-potty.

"I'm sorry, but . . ." Katie began.

"Here, I've got the money ready for you, exact change," the man with the small tree said.

The woman in the blue and yellow checked coat was growing very impatient. "I really would like to get my Christmas tree to my car."

"Is there a coffee shop anywhere near here

that Joshie could use?" the mother asked Katie.

Too late! A yellow puddle formed at Joshie's feet. He started howling.

The man with the small Christmas tree dropped his money on the counter. "I've got to go," he told Katie. "Merry Christmas."

Katie sighed. "Whatever," she murmured, as she put the money in the cash register, and went off to find someone to carry a Christmas tree to a car.

Chapter 8

A few minutes later, everything had calmed down. The woman in the checked coat had driven away with her tree. Joshie and his mother had gone off in search of dry clothes. And there was no one waiting in line at the cash register. Things were so quiet, Katie could hear Christmas music playing from speakers set up around the tree farm.

"Oh Christmas tree, oh Christmas tree, of all the trees most lovely!" Katie sang along with the music. Her Christmas spirit was back. After all, she was only cranky Holly on the outside. She was still jolly Katie on the inside.

That was a problem. For all she knew

Grandma and Nick were looking for her right now. And they wouldn't be able to find her anywhere.

Katie looked hopefully around for any sign of the magic wind's return. Unfortunately she didn't see any wild tornados coming her way. What she did see, though, was a father and his two little girls.

This family stood out from the other shoppers at the farm. They weren't all bundled up in gloves and heavy coats. Their coats were thin. The kids had their hands shoved in their pockets to keep them warm.

"I'm sorry. I know how much you want a tree," Katie heard the father say sadly. "But even the small ones are too expensive. We just can't spare the money right now."

"It's okay, Daddy," Katie heard one of the girls say. "It's still Christmas, even without a tree."

Now *Katie* was the one who felt sad. A Christmas without a tree? She just couldn't let that happen!

Before she could stop the words from leaving her lips, Katie blurted out. "If you want this tree, you can have it." She pointed to a nice short full tree.

The father stopped and stared at her. "Do you mean that?"

Katie looked at the two little girls. They had big smiles on their faces.

"Of course," Katie said. "It's Christmas. Everyone should have a tree. Go ahead. Please, I want you to take it."

"Thank you! Thank you!" The two girls cheered.

"You are the nicest person I've ever met," the father told Katie. "You'll never know what a wonderful thing you've just done."

Katie smiled. For once, the magic wind had changed her into a person who could do something nice for someone else. How great was that!?

"Here, I'll help you carry the tree to your

car," Katie said, feeling more and more of the Christmas spirit coming over her.

"Holly, you are the sweetest lady ever!" one of the little girls exclaimed.

If she only knew the truth, Katie thought. But she didn't say that. Instead, she said, "Thank you."

After Katie helped to load the Christmas tree onto the roof of their old car, she began to walk back to the farm. She hadn't gotten very far when she felt a cool breeze blowing on the back of her neck.

Katie knew what that meant. The magic wind had returned!

Sure enough, in a flash, that cool breeze soon turned into an icy, powerful tornado. A tornado was spinning just around Katie. She shut her eyes, and tried her hardest not to be blown away.

And then it stopped. Just like that.

The magic wind was gone. And Katie Kazoo was back.

So was Holly. She was standing right next to Katie. And boy, was she confused.

"What am I doing out here in the parking lot?" Holly asked Katie.

"You were helping a man and his two daughters with their tree," Katie told her.

"Why would I do that?" Holly wondered.

"To be nice," Katie explained.

Holly laughed. "Yeah, right," she said.

"No, you *were* nice. One of the girls even said you were the nicest lady ever," Katie told Holly.

Holly shook her head. "You're a weird kid," she said. "No one would ever say that about me." Then she thought for a minute. "Or maybe once they did. I kind of remember something like that."

"Well it *was* really kind of me . . . I mean of *you* to give them that tree for free," Katie told Holly.

"I gave them a what? For *what*?" Holly asked Katie. She looked upset.

"That family didn't have much money," Katie told her. "And they couldn't afford a tree so I . . . I mean you . . ."

"What was I thinking?" Holly interrupted Katie. "I would never give a tree away. What if my boss finds out?"

"Your boss?" Katie asked her.

"Yeah," Holly said. "You don't think I own this place, do you?"

Katie hadn't really thought about it.

"He likes to *sell* trees," Holly continued. "He might fire me for giving one away."

Katie gulped. Holly might lose her job. And if she did, it would all be Katie's fault.

This was *soooo* not good.

But Katie wasn't sure what she could do to help Holly. She wasn't even sure if she *should* help. After all, she'd tried to help the poor family, and look what a mess that turned out to be.

Her only hope was that no one had seen her give the tree to that family. Maybe it would just remain their little secret.

★ ★ ★

No such luck! As soon as she and Holly got back from the parking lot, her grandmother was the first person to greet them.

"You are such a nice person," Katie's

grandmother told Holly. "Giving that tree to that out-of-luck father and his kids was truly the real Christmas spirit!"

Holly didn't answer. She just glared in Katie's direction. Then she turned to Nick, who was leaning against a medium-sized tree. "You gonna buy that?" she asked him.

"I sure am!" Nick said. He reached into his pocket, and handed Holly the money. "Thanks for keeping my secret," he added in a whisper.

Holly looked at him strangely. "What secret?" she asked.

Katie heard Nick say in a very low voice, "Don't you remember? The surprise for—." Nick nodded in Katie's direction.

"Huh?" Holly asked. She had no idea what he was talking about.

"You sure can keep a secret," Nick told her. Then, as he started to carry the tree back to the car, he called out, "Merry Christmas!"

"Whatever," Holly replied with a sigh.

Chapter 9

"Grandma told me about that woman who works at the tree farm," Katie's mom said that night. Katie's whole family was spending the evening together, decorating the new Christmas tree. "What a nice thing to do!"

"What are you talking about?" Katie asked nervously. Did her mother already know about Holly?

"I called your mom at the bookstore after we got home and told her how that kind woman gave a Christmas tree to a poor family," Katie's grandmother piped in. She placed a teddy bear ornament on the tree and smiled happily.

But Katie wasn't happy at all. "Why did you

54

do that?" she asked.

Katie's mom look surprised. "Grandma was just so impressed with what she did," her mom said.

"We all were," Nick added. He tossed a handful of tinsel onto a few of the lower branches. "Holly seemed so grumpy. But she had the true Christmas spirit."

"Well, I don't think we should spread that story any further," Katie told everyone.

"Don't be silly," Katie's mom said. "I told Louie and he told everyone who came into the pizzeria about it."

"Oh no!" Katie said.

"What's the matter?" Katie's dad asked. "Don't you think what that woman did was a great thing?"

"Sure, *I* do," Katie said. "But maybe her boss won't. I mean, he makes a living selling Christmas trees."

"I don't think he'll mind," Nick said. "It was only one little tree. How could anyone get mad at someone for giving a poor family a Christmas tree?"

"Besides, when the story gets out, everyone will want to buy their trees at that farm," Katie's father said. "People like to give their business to places that do nice things for people."

"You really think so?" Katie asked her dad.

"Oh, definitely," he answered.

A big smile formed on Katie's face. She had just gotten a great idea! Quickly, she leaped up from the pile of tinsel and ornaments around her.

"Where are you going, Kit Kat?" her mother asked. "We still haven't placed the star on the top of the tree."

"I'll be right back," Katie told everyone. "I just have a quick phone call to make."

Chapter 10

Katie stared at the Saturday morning headline in the *Cherrydale News* excitedly. "Tree Salesperson Brightens Family's Christmas," it said. The news story reported that an anonymous source had called the paper and told them the story about Holly and the poor family.

Katie knew the anonymous source very well. *She* was the anonymous source! Katie hoped that her phone call would help keep Holly out of trouble. Holly deserved her job. She worked really hard at the tree farm. Now Katie could understand why sometimes Holly got grumpy. The place was like a zoo at times! Katie knew

that first hand. After all, she'd been Holly. At least for a little while.

Honk! Honk! Just then, a car horn honked outside. Katie leaped up and ran for the door.

"It's Suzanne's mom, Grandma," Katie shouted out.

"Have fun working on the scenery for the play," her grandmother called back from the kitchen.

"Thanks!" Katie shouted as she raced out the door to the car.

⋆ ⋆ ⋆

"Good morning," Katie said, as she opened

the car door and climbed in beside Suzanne in the backseat.

"Good morning," Mrs. Lock greeted her.

"Hi, Katie," Suzanne said.

"Hi! Hi!" Heather shouted from her car seat.

"Hi, Heather," Katie said.

Suzanne shot Katie a look.

"What?" Katie asked. "Can't I say hi to her?"

Suzanne folded her arms across her chest. "Do whatever you want," she said.

"We have just one stop to make before I drop you girls off at the Community Center," Mrs. Lock told Katie. "I want to get a wreath for our front door at that tree farm I read about in the paper this morning."

Katie smiled. Her plan was working. At least with Mrs. Lock.

"They have beautiful wreaths," Katie said. "Nick bought a really pretty one for me as a surprise. But I should warn you, not all of the wreaths have price tags."

Suzanne looked at her strangely. "What were you doing, examining every wreath?"

"No. It's just that Nick wanted a specific wreath. But that one didn't have a price on it, so I . . . I mean, so *Holly* . . ." Katie stammered, trying to come up with a way to explain what had happened at the tree farm.

But Suzanne didn't really care about wreaths or Christmas tree farms. She cared about what *she* was going to be doing today.

"While you're busy painting at the Community Center, I'll be running around," she said. "I've got to get all the lighting cues right. And then I have to make sure the costumes are being sewn. And then I have to stand backstage during rehearsal to make sure all the actors are saying the right lines."

"Wow, that's a big job," Katie told her.

"I know," Suzanne said. "The whole play depends on me."

Katie doubted that was true. A play was a team effort. Everyone was equally important.

"Mama! Mama!" Heather shouted out suddenly.

"Oh, how cute. She's practicing her lines," Mrs. Lock cooed.

Suzanne sighed heavily. "See what I mean?" she whispered to Katie.

Now Heather was bouncing up and down in her car seat. It was obvious Suzanne's baby sister wasn't practicing anything. She just didn't like being in the car seat.

"Out!" Heather shrieked. "Want out! Mama. Mama."

"Okay, Heatherkins," Mrs. Lock said. "One more minute. I just have to park the car."

"Ma—" Heather started. But Suzanne stuffed a sippy cup in her hands before she could make another sound.

"Thanks, Suzanne," Mrs. Lock said. She pulled the car into the parking lot and turned off the motor. "Okay, Heather, we're going to let you out now."

Katie got out of the car, and watched as

Mrs. Lock unhooked Heather from her car seat. A moment later, the four of them were walking toward the tree farm.

Suddenly, Katie's stomach started doing flip flops. She was really nervous. What if her plan hadn't worked? What if Holly wasn't working at the tree farm any more? What if by saving one family's Christmas, Katie had ruined Holly's?

There were definitely a lot of people at the Christmas tree farm. Katie could see that. There were people looking at trees, wreaths, and decorations. There were people drinking hot cider and eating chestnuts. And there were lots of people waiting around the cash register. But Katie didn't see Holly anywhere.

Then, Katie heard a customer near the cash register say, "Merry Christmas."

And a moment later, she heard a familiar voice say, "Whatever."

"Holly!" Katie shouted out excitedly.

Holly poked her head up over the crowd. "Oh, it's you again," she said.

"I'm back with my friends," Katie told her. "The news article made you sound really nice. They wanted to buy their Christmas wreath from you."

"That's what all these people are saying," Holly said. "We've been mobbed all morning."

"That's good, right?" Katie asked her. "I mean, you didn't get fired."

"No, I didn't get fired," Holly said. "My boss loves all the extra business. He even made me Employee of the Week." She pointed to the special star-shaped pin she was wearing. Nevertheless, Holly's mouth was frozen in her usual frown. She did not look like a happy Employee of the Week.

"My boss also gave me a Christmas gift," Holly continued. "He's never done that before."

"That's so nice," Katie said. "What did he give you?"

For the first time, Holly cracked a smile. A genuine, happy smile. "You're not going to believe this," she told Katie. "He gave me a Christmas tree. How funny is that? What would make him think that after a whole day of working here, I'd want to come home to a tree?"

Katie laughed. Holly couldn't fool her. She might sound tough, but her smile said it all. Holly liked coming home to that tree very, very much.

Chapter 11

"Katie, don't use so much paint," Suzanne scolded, as she walked over to look at the scenery.

Katie shook her head. She was getting tired of Suzanne bossing people around. She'd been hearing her order people around all morning. They had to sing louder, dance in a straighter line, and even stay away from the donuts at the snack table. Katie had had enough.

"I'm using just the right amount of paint," Katie snapped back. "These trees look great!"

Suzanne glared at Katie. "You can't talk to me like that. I'm the stage manager."

"The *student* stage manager," Katie

reminded her. "Mr. Porter is the real stage manager."

"I'm real, too!" Suzanne shouted. She stomped away angrily.

"A real *pain*," Katie murmured under her breath. She put some more green paint on her brush and went back to work.

It took a few minutes, but soon Katie was feeling happier again. It was hard to stay upset for too long, especially when the cast was rehearsing the songs. All of the music was so happy.

"Trains, and trucks, and a baby doll," they sang. "There are children who would love us all."

Their voices sounded so cheerful. And they blended so nicely together. Until suddenly, someone hit a real clinker of a note.

"Suzanne!" Mr. Porter shouted out. "You're not supposed to be singing along."

"I just thought the song needed to be louder and have more voices," Suzanne told him.

"Not your voice," Mr. Porter told her.

Katie bit her lip and tried not to laugh.

"I mean, um, I mean, stage managers don't sing. We manage," Mr. Porter explained.

"Oh, right," Suzanne said. She sounded a little disappointed. "What do you want me to manage now?"

"How about standing backstage and handing cups of water to the dancers in between songs?" Mr. Porter suggested.

"That doesn't sound very important," Suzanne told him.

"Oh, it is," Mr. Porter assured her. "The dancers can't do their best if they're thirsty."

"That's true," Suzanne said.

As Suzanne hurried off for the water and plastic cups, Mr. Porter walked over to Katie and some of the others.

"That tree looks great!" he complimented Katie.

"Thanks," Katie said. "I've been working on the scenery all morning. It's almost finished."

"And just in time," Mr. Porter said. "The show opens in three days."

"Are you going to be ready?" Katie asked him.

"I hope so," Mr. Porter said with a smile.

At that moment, Suzanne came running across the stage with the pitcher of water in her hands.

"Watch out, stage manager coming through," she shouted. "This water is heavy . . . whoaaaaa!"

Suzanne tripped over a large box onstage. The pitcher slipped out of her hands. Water spilled everywhere.

"Who left that box there?" Suzanne demanded as she stood in the middle of the big puddle of water.

"I did," Mr. Newman, the director, shouted. He came bounding up toward the stage. "It's supposed to be there. It's the jack-in-the-box."

"Oh, sorry," Suzanne said. "I didn't see it."

"Obviously," Mr. Newman said. "And now

you've ruined it. The cardboard is sopping wet."

Katie looked at Mr. Newman. Then she looked at Mr. Porter. They both seemed really angry with Suzanne.

Katie felt really bad for her friend. She

hadn't meant to mess up. It had just been an accident.

"I'm almost done with this tree," Katie shouted out suddenly. "If you can find another box, I can paint it really quickly."

"Great, Katie!" Mr. Porter said. Then he turned to Suzanne. "Why don't you go get some paper towels and dry up the stage? We don't want anyone else falling here today."

"Yes, sir," Suzanne said meekly.

Katie grabbed her paintbrush and hurried to put the finishing strokes on her Christmas tree. As Suzanne walked by, she gave her friend an encouraging smile.

"Are you okay?" Katie asked Suzanne.

"Of course I'm okay," Suzanne told her. "It was just a little water."

"I know, it's just that Mr. Newman is kind of scary."

Suzanne shrugged. "He's not so bad." Then she looked at the tree Katie was painting. "You'd better get back to work," she ordered. "You've got a lot to do. Mr. Newman and Mr. Porter will want that tree and the jack-in-the-box completely painted before we leave today."

Grrrr. Now Katie was really mad. She had volunteered to help Suzanne out of a big mess, and now Suzanne was bossing her around. For a minute, Katie thought about putting down her brush and walking out of there. Let Suzanne paint the jack-in-the-box.

But Katie couldn't do that. Suzanne wasn't a very talented artist. She probably wouldn't do a very good job. And it was important that the scenery look good. After all, Katie wasn't doing this for Suzanne. She was doing this for the play. She had to keep painting. But that didn't mean she had to keep listening to Suzanne.

"You go clean up your mess," Katie told her. "And leave the painting to me. I know what I'm doing."

Chapter 12

"So, how is the play going down at the Community Center?" Jeremy asked Katie. It was late Saturday afternoon. Katie had come to Jeremy's house to help him celebrate the first night of Hanukkah.

"Well, Suzanne was there . . ." Katie began.

Jeremy laughed. "That's all you have to say."

"Totally. You should have seen her. She . . ." Katie began. Then she stopped herself. This was the holiday season. It was a time to be nice. "Well, she's trying," she added quickly. "It's a tough job."

"How does your scenery look?" Jeremy asked Katie.

"I think it's pretty good, actually," Katie said. "I have to go back tomorrow and finish up a few things on the last Christmas tree."

"You're a good artist," Jeremy told her. "Suzanne's really lucky to have you helping out with the play."

"Thanks," Katie said.

She sat down on the couch and looked around Jeremy's living room. There was a blue and silver banner hanging across the wall that said "Happy Hanukkah." A silver menorah had been placed near the window. It had two candles in it.

"I thought this was the *first* night of Hanukkah," she said.

"It is," Jeremy told her. "The candle in the middle is the *shemash*, the helper candle. We use it to light the other ones."

"Oh. I forgot. I haven't done this since last year when I came over for Hanukkah," Katie said. "Are we going to play that game tonight? The one with the top and the chocolate candies?"

"Definitely," Jeremy answered. "We always play the dreidel game on Hanukkah."

"You're so lucky that your holiday starts tonight," Katie said, with more than a touch of jealousy. "I have to wait until Thursday night for Christmas Eve. All those presents are sitting there under the tree, just waiting for me. And all I can do is stare at them."

Jeremy nodded. "I know what you mean. My parents have wrapped all of my gifts for the whole eight days of Hanukkah. They're sitting in the basement on the ping-pong table.

I really want to just take a peek at one or two of them."

"Don't you dare," Mrs. Fox said, as she entered the room. She had a big smile on her face. "That will ruin the surprise. Now, are you two ready to light the menorah and get this holiday started?"

"Oh yeah!" Jeremy cheered. "Where's Dad?"

"Right here," Mr. Fox said, as he came up the stairs from the basement. "I was just getting your first present."

"Okay, are we ready?" Mrs. Fox asked the kids.

Katie and Jeremy nodded. Then Katie watched as Mrs. Fox used the *shemash* to light the candle on the end of the menorah—the one that was for the first night.

While she lit the candle, Jeremy said a prayer in Hebrew.

"I didn't know you could speak Hebrew," Katie said to him.

"I can't," Jeremy admitted. "I just know that one prayer."

"And you did it beautifully," Mrs. Fox said. She handed Jeremy a small box. "Happy first night of Hanukkah."

"Thanks," Jeremy said excitedly.

"Don't think we forgot you, Katie," Mrs. Fox

said. She handed Katie a box as well.

"Wow! Thank you," Katie exclaimed. She hadn't been expecting a present. "You open yours first," she told Jeremy.

Jeremy opened his gift box. He pulled out something that looked like a watch without the band. "How do I wear this watch?" he asked.

"It's not a watch," his dad told him. "It's a pedometer."

"A pedo-*what*?" Jeremy asked.

"A pedometer," Mr. Fox repeated. "You put it in your pocket. It tells you how many steps you walk or run in a day."

"How does it do that?" Jeremy asked.

Mr. Fox shrugged. "I have no idea. I just know it works."

Jeremy put the pedometer in his jeans pocket and began to walk around the room. "One, two, three, four, five, six," he said as he counted his steps. Then he pulled the pedometer out of his pocket. "Wow. It says six steps. This thing really does work."

"Wait until you use it a whole day," Katie told him. "I'll bet you walk ten thousand steps. Maybe even a million steps on the days you have soccer practice!"

"Cool!" Jeremy exclaimed. "Now you open your present, Katie."

Katie didn't have to be told twice. She opened the box. Inside was a purple, plastic top with Hebrew letters on it. There was also a package of chocolate coins covered in gold foil. "A dreidel!" Katie exclaimed.

"And chocolate money," Jeremy reminded her. "Don't forget the chocolate."

"I could never forget chocolate," Katie said with a smile. "I love chocolate."

"I remembered how much you liked playing the dreidel game last year, so we thought you'd like one of your own," Mrs. Fox said.

"I love it!" Katie exclaimed. "Thank you so much."

"Can we play dreidel right now?" Jeremy asked his mom.

"Sure. The potato pancakes have to fry a little longer, anyway," she answered.

"Let's use your dreidel," Jeremy told Katie. "You can spin first."

"Thanks," Katie said. She sat down on the floor and gave her top a good spin.

"I love Hanukkah!" Jeremy exclaimed as they watched the top spin around and around.

"I love this whole season!" Katie agreed.

Chapter 13

What Katie *didn't* love, however, was working on the play with Suzanne. But that was exactly what she was stuck doing on Sunday afternoon. And listening to Suzanne boss everyone around was really getting old.

"James, you have to wear your elf hat," Katie heard Suzanne insisting to one of the actors in the play. "How else will the audience know you're an elf?"

"There's no audience here, Suzanne. It's just a rehearsal," James answered her. "And besides, I'm not even in this scene. I'm going out in the hall to make a phone call."

"Oh," Suzanne said. "Well, you should

wear your hat, anyway. That way you'll stay in character!"

James shook his head and ignored Suzanne. Katie didn't blame him. Suzanne might be her best friend, but she was also a real pain in the neck.

"Make sure that sleigh is strong and won't break," Suzanne told Henry, the man who was building Santa's sleigh. "My little sister is going to be sitting on that during the play."

Katie was surprised at that. Suzanne usually didn't care what happened to Heather. But of course, right now, having a little sister in the play gave her a chance to boss someone around.

"Don't worry, kiddo," Henry said. "Your sister will be safe on this."

Katie could tell from the look on her face that Suzanne didn't like being called "kiddo." That didn't sound like something you would call a stage manager. But Suzanne didn't say anything. After all, Henry was a grown-up.

"Could you guys paint a little faster?" Suzanne asked, as she walked over to where Katie and the other scenery people were working. "This forest is taking longer to paint than a real one takes to grow."

Grrrr. That made Katie really mad. She leaped up, and waved her paintbrush at Suzanne. "If you think it's so easy, why don't you try it?"

Suzanne jumped back. "I can't believe you did that!" she yelled at Katie. "You got paint on my sweater!"

"And on your face, too," one of the other painters pointed out. "And in your hair." She began to laugh.

Soon all the scenery painters were laughing. "A little more paint on your face and you could stand in the background and be one of the trees," one of them said.

Suzanne's eyes became angry, little slits. She glared at Katie. "Thanks a lot!"

"Oh, come on," Katie said. "What's the big

deal? We have paint all over us. And we're not complaining."

"You're *supposed* to be a mess," Suzanne told her. "You're scenery people. But I'm in charge!"

"Suzanne!" Mr. Porter shouted.

Suzanne took a deep breath, and smoothed out her sweater. "I have to go." She tried to sound very dignified. "Obviously, Mr. Porter has something very important for me to do."

Suzanne walked across the stage. "Yes, Mr. Porter, here I am."

"I need you to go make some more peanut butter and jelly sandwiches for the cast," he told her.

Katie choked back a laugh. That didn't sound very important. At least not to her.

But Suzanne said, "Yes sir, Mr. Porter. I know how important it is to keep the cast from being hungry."

Katie laughed. What a very Suzanne thing to say!

⭐ ⭐ ⭐

A few minutes later, as Katie was helping to arrange some of the wooden trees backstage, Suzanne came walking back with a tray full of sandwiches.

"Come and get it!" she called out to the cast.

The singers, dancers, and actors all came running over. They were so anxious to eat the sandwiches that they nearly pushed Suzanne over. She had to jump out of the way to keep from getting trampled. As she jumped, she brushed against one of the trees.

"Suzanne!" Katie shouted. "That one was still wet."

Suzanne looked down at her sweater. Sure enough, another streak of green paint was there. "It wasn't my fault," she told Katie.

"It wasn't mine, either," Katie said. "You fix it."

But before Suzanne could answer, Mr. Porter called out her name. "Suzanne, a few members of the cast are going to run through the scene in Santa's Workshop. I need you to stand backstage and make sure they get their lines right."

"Yes, Mr. Porter," Suzanne said. She picked up her script and walked over to the side of the stage, just behind the curtain.

"Okay, cast," Mr. Newman shouted. "Action."

"It's almost Christmas," one of the elf actors said loudly from behind a workbench. "We have to finish these toys quickly."

"I wonder how Santa knows where all these toys belong," said another.

"Santa's smart," a third actor said.

"Well, one thing's for sure," said a fourth. "The kids will love these toys. They're perfect!"

Then the music began to play. The actors playing the elves started to dance in a circle. They spun each other by the elbows and kicked their feet in the air.

From where she was working, Katie could see Suzanne backstage. She was kicking her feet in time to the music. When it came time for the dancers to spin each other, Suzanne spun around.

Oh no! Katie watched, her eyes opening wide in horror, as Suzanne lost her balance and grabbed for a long rope . . . the rope for the curtain!

Woosh! The curtain came down, right in the middle of the dance. *Bam!* Two of the dancers bashed into each other.

"Ouch!" the dancers cried out.

"SUZANNE!" Mr. Porter exclaimed.

"Get that girl out of here!" Mr. Newman shouted.

Suzanne looked like she was about to cry.

Suddenly, Katie felt kind of bad for Suzanne. No matter how bossy she had been, she didn't deserve to be yelled at like that. It wasn't like she'd dropped the curtain on purpose.

★ ★ ★

A little while later, Katie found herself in the Community Center lobby with Suzanne. The girls were waiting for Mrs. Lock to pick them up from rehearsal.

"Mr. Newman sure was mean," Katie said, trying to make Suzanne feel better.

But Suzanne didn't seem upset at all.

"Directors can be like that," she said. "Besides, Mr. Porter and I had a long talk. He gave me a new job. It's better suited to my talents."

Katie wasn't sure what talents Suzanne was talking about. "What are you going to be doing?"

"You'll see on Tuesday night," Suzanne told her. "It's a surprise."

Chapter 14

On Tuesday night, Suzanne was the first person Katie and her friends saw when they arrived at the Community Center for the show. She was in the lobby selling candy and soda.

"This is your big job?" Jeremy asked. "The one you were bragging about all day in school?"

Suzanne nodded. "I'm in charge of the refreshments. That's a very important job. These snacks raise a lot of money for the Community Center."

"I'll have two boxes of chocolate-covered raisins," George said.

"That will be two dollars," Suzanne told him.

George handed Suzanne the money. "Thanks," he said.

"How is this job suited to your talents?" Katie asked her.

"Well, I'm a model, right?" Suzanne reminded Katie.

Katie didn't say anything. Suzanne wasn't really a model. She just took modeling classes. But Suzanne always insisted that was the same thing. So Katie just shrugged.

"I *am* a model," Suzanne insisted. "And models do a lot of advertising, on TV and in magazines. I'm advertising this candy, by telling people what we have. I'm the spokesmodel for all this candy."

Katie sighed. It was incredible the way Suzanne could turn anything around to make her look good. "You're amazing, Suzanne," she said.

"Thanks." Suzanne smiled brightly.

"How does Heather look in her costume?" Emma W. asked Suzanne.

"Not as great as I look in this dress," Suzanne said, spinning around so the kids

could see her new red and green dress. "But of course, she doesn't need to look that nice. She's only on stage for a minute or two. I'm going to be out here being a spokesmodel before the show and during the intermission."

"You do look pretty," Katie assured Suzanne.

"I'll be back at intermission for more candy," George assured her.

"Try our peanut brittle," Suzanne suggested. She flashed George a model-y smile. "It's delicious."

"We'd better get inside if we want good seats," Jeremy said.

"Yeah. We'll see you at intermission, Suzanne," Katie said.

"I'll be here during intermission and all during tomorrow night's show, too," Suzanne assured her. "This is the perfect job for me."

※ ※ ※

"That was a really good show," Katie said later that evening, as she, Emma W., George, and Jeremy drove home with Katie's grandmother and Nick.

"It was okay," George said. "Except for when Heather cried."

"They probably shouldn't have used a real baby in the show," Emma W. said. "A doll would have been better."

"Definitely," Jeremy said. "And I'm sure tomorrow Suzanne will be telling everyone that."

The kids all laughed. They all knew Suzanne loved to say "I told you so."

"Your scenery looked beautiful," Emma told Katie. "I really felt like we were in the North Pole."

"Thanks," Katie said. "That's exactly how we wanted it to look."

"Wouldn't it be great to be an elf in Santa's Workshop?" George asked the other kids.

"Too bad that's impossible," Katie said.

"Is it?" Katie's grandma asked the kids.

"Of course it is, Grandma," Katie said. "We live in Cherrydale. That's pretty far from the North Pole."

"What if I told you that I could take you to Santa's Workshop?" Nick said.

The kids laughed again.

"I'll tell you what," Nick said. "Tomorrow is your last school day before vacation. When school lets out, I'll pick you kids up and take you to Santa's Workshop."

"You can't *really* do that," Katie said.

"Sure I can," Nick told her. "Anything is possible at Christmastime."

Chapter 15

"You can't get to the North Pole in a car," Matthew Weber told Nick the next afternoon.

Matthew was Emma W.'s little brother. He had tagged along with Katie and her friends on their North Pole Experience. That was what Nick was calling this exciting after-school trip.

"Well, how else would we get to the North Pole?" Nick asked Matthew. "We can't walk there."

"You have to fly," Matthew said. "In a sleigh, pulled by reindeer."

"Or at least in a plane," George added.

"Ho, ho, ho," Nick laughed. "I think this old

car will get us there just fine."

Katie didn't really think Nick was taking them to the North Pole. But he sounded so sure of himself that Katie didn't know what to believe.

"We're almost there," Nick said. "So you kids had better bundle up. It's plenty cold up at the North Pole."

Emma W. turned to her little brother. "You'd better put on your hat and gloves, Matty," she said. "And don't forget your scarf."

"If I put all that on, how will Santa recognize me?" Matthew asked Emma.

"He'll just know," Emma assured him. "Santa's smart that way."

"How many miles have we gone so far?" Katie asked Jeremy.

"I don't know," he said.

"Don't you have your pedometer with you?" she wondered.

Jeremy nodded. "It only works when you walk, not when you drive."

"Besides, these are magical miles," Nick said. "You can't measure a trip to the North Pole in a regular way."

Katie looked over at Matthew. She could tell the first-grader was soaking in everything Nick said. She didn't want to tell him that Nick was only teasing. So she said, "Everything about Christmas is magical. Don't you think so, Matthew?"

Matthew nodded. "Are we gonna meet the reindeer?" he asked Nick. "I want to see Rudolph's red nose."

"I don't know if we'll see Rudolph," Nick told Matthew. "He might be resting up. It's a big job leading a sleigh on Christmas Eve. But I think we'll be able to see some other reindeer."

"Cool," Matthew said excitedly.

"Do you guys know what you call a reindeer wearing earmuffs?" George asked.

"What?" Jeremy wondered.

"You can call him anything," George answered. "He can't hear you!"

Everyone laughed. Especially Nick. He let out a hearty, "Ho, ho, ho."

A few minutes later, Nick turned off the main road. Suddenly, the kids found themselves driving through a snowy winter wonderland. Crystal-like icicles hung from the trees. And the smell of pine drifted in through the car windows.

"We're here!" Matthew squealed excitedly. "This looks just like the North Pole in my picture book."

"You're right, Matthew," Nick said. He parked the car and opened the door. "Welcome to the North Pole, kids!"

As Katie stepped out of the car, she saw a big red and white striped sign. It read: North Pole Winter Fun Park.

"It's an amusement p . . ." Katie started. But then she stopped herself when she caught a glimpse of Matthew's face. His eyes were open wide. He was so excited. He thought they were at the real North Pole. Katie didn't want to ruin that. "It's amazing!" she corrected herself quickly.

A small man with big, brown eyes walked over to greet them. He was wearing a pair of green overalls, a red shirt, and a red and green ski jacket.

"Welcome to the North Pole, kids," he greeted them. "I'm Mr. Frost. I'll be your guide to Santa's Workshop."

"Wow!" Matthew said. "We're going to the workshop!"

"Are we going on a sleigh ride, too?" Katie asked Mr. Frost excitedly. Then she blushed. She sounded just like a little kid.

But Katie's friends were just as excited as she was.

"You sure will," Mr. Frost assured her.

"I've never seen a real reindeer," Jeremy said.

"Me neither," Emma added.

"I need some hot chocolate," George said. "It's cold up here at the North Pole."

Mr. Frost smiled. "It sure is. There's hot chocolate over there in that little cottage. Why don't you go over and get yourself some?"

The kids all looked up at Nick.

"Is it okay?" Katie asked him.

"Go ahead," Nick replied. "Mr. Frost and I have to arrange for that reindeer ride you want."

"Are we going to fly in a sleigh?" Matthew asked.

"We won't be flying," Mr. Frost told him. "Only Santa can do that. But you'll be in a sleigh and reindeer will be pulling you."

"That sounds fun, too," Emma W. said.

As Nick and Mr. Frost spoke, Katie and her friends trudged through the snow to the little cottage. It looked just like a gingerbread house, with candy canes around the windowsills, and gumdrop designs on the doors. And when they opened the door, the smell of sweet hot chocolate came blasting out at them.

"This place is amazing!" Jeremy exclaimed,

as he hurried over and poured himself a big cup of hot chocolate.

"I could eat this whole house," George said. "If the gumdrops weren't wood and the candy canes weren't made of plaster, that is."

Katie giggled. Everything George said always came out sounding so funny.

Suddenly, the kids heard bells outside the little cottage. Katie ran over to the window to see what was going on out there. Her face lit up with excitement.

"Those are sleigh bells!" she exclaimed. "And the sleigh is being pulled by three real reindeer. You should see how huge their antlers are!"

The kids all rushed outside for a closer look. Nick was standing beside the reindeer. He was feeding them sugar cubes.

"Can I try?" Katie asked.

"Sure," Nick said. He handed her a sugar cube.

As Katie held her hand up to the reindeer's mouth, she noticed something odd. "He has fur on his lips," she said.

Nick nodded. "That protects his mouth from the cold. You'd need a fur coat over your mouth, too, if you lived at the North Pole."

"That's why I have my scarf pulled over my mouth," Katie told Nick.

Nick smiled. "Exactly. But you have to admit, a reindeer would look pretty funny in a wool scarf."

Katie giggled at the thought of it.

"Reindeer are so amazing," Emma W. said.

"You haven't seen anything yet," Nick told her. "Wait until you're dashing through the snow, in a reindeer open sleigh . . ."

The kids all laughed at Nick's funny version of "Jingle Bells."

The driver of the sleigh, a tall, skinny man in a long overcoat, hopped down from his seat. He tipped his hat and bowed to Katie. "Pleased to meet you. I'm Tom."

"I'm Katie," she answered.

"Hi, Katie," Tom said. "Let me help you up." Tom lifted her into the sleigh.

A few minutes later, Katie and her friends were all snuggled together under a thick, wool blanket. Nick was sitting up front with Tom.

"Is everybody ready?" Tom asked.

"Yeah!" The kids all cheered at once.

"Then let's giddyup!" Tom said.

Chapter 16

Woosh! The wind blew hard as the sleigh made its way down the path. Katie was glad the blanket blocked out this wind. That meant it was a real wind—not the magic kind. Katie didn't want to miss a minute of this sleigh ride because of a silly switcheroo!

"I feel just like Santa," George said. "Except we're not flying."

"I'm cold," Matthew told his big sister.

"We all are," Emma told him. Then she pulled him a little closer to keep him warm. "But think about the reindeer. They're not even wearing coats."

"They have thick fur," Tom reminded Emma.

"They're plenty comfortable in this weather.
Don't you worry."

Nick said, "Imagine pulling a sleigh with
Santa and a bundle of toys all around the world
on Christmas Eve. *Phew.*"

"I think Santa's job is even harder," Katie told Nick. "He's the one carrying that heavy sack and squeezing down chimneys. The reindeer are just running in the air."

"I've never run through the air," Emma said. "Maybe it's harder than regular running."

"I can name all the reindeer," Matthew shouted out. "There's Dasher, and Dancer, Prancer and Vixen, Comet, and Cupid, Donner, Blitzen, and Rudolph."

"Exactly," Katie told Matthew with a smile. "And they all pull the sleigh as a team. But there's only one Santa."

"I love getting presents from Santa!" cried Matthew.

Katie and her friends all laughed at that. Little kids could be so funny sometimes. They were also right a lot of times. After all, who doesn't love getting presents?

★ ★ ★

The sleigh ride was over way too soon. Before they knew it, the kids were back at the gingerbread shack.

"Did you have a good time?" Mr. Frost asked the group.

"The best," Jeremy assured him.

"It was amazing," Katie agreed.

"The reindeer were so fast," George added.

"I have to pee," Matthew said.

Emma W. laughed. Then she turned to Mr. Frost. "Where's the bathroom?"

Mr. Frost pointed off to the left. "In the building just behind the candy cane maze."

"The candy cane what?" Katie asked.

"It's a giant maze," Mr. Frost explained. "All the paths are marked with huge metal candy canes and licorice sticks. And at the end of the maze is Santa's Workshop. He just might be in there working with the elves."

"That sounds like fun," George said.

"It is," Mr. Frost assured him. "But I'm warning you, it's pretty tricky!"

"Not for me," Jeremy said. "I'm great at mazes."

"Give it a try," Mr. Frost told him.

"All right!" Jeremy cheered. He ran off. Emma W., Matthew, and George followed closely behind him.

"You want to come, too, Nick?" Katie asked.

Nick shook his head. "These old bones need some hot chocolate."

Katie frowned. Soon, Tom and Mr. Frost would go back to work. That meant Nick would be all by himself.

"Do you want me to stay here with you?"

"No, Katie," Nick said. "I'm fine. You go with your friends. I'll meet you back at the cottage."

"Okay," Katie said. She didn't have to be told twice. She took off in the same direction as her friends. "Hey! Wait for me!" Katie called. But her friends were too far ahead to hear her.

Brrr. Suddenly, Katie felt a cold breeze on the back of her neck. This might not be the real North Pole, but it sure felt like it. She pulled her scarf a little tighter around her neck.

But that didn't help. A little wool scarf

couldn't protect Katie from this wind. After all, the breeze she felt was no ordinary wind. It was the magic wind!

The magic wind picked up speed after that. It blew harder and harder, circling around Katie like an icy tornado. It was so cold, Katie was afraid she was going to freeze into a human snowgirl.

And then it stopped. Just like that.

The magic wind was gone. And so was Katie. She'd turned into someone new.

But who?

Chapter 17

Katie blinked twice and looked around. She was standing in the snow at the North Pole Winter Fun Park. Right in front of her was the little gingerbread house where she and her friends had gotten hot chocolate. Okay, so now she knew *where* she was. But she still didn't know *who* she was.

It was weird. Although Katie was outside, she didn't feel cold right now. In fact, she was kind of warm and comfortable. Like she was cuddled under a wool blanket. But she wasn't under a blanket.

Katie looked down at her feet. Uh-oh! Instead of her pink and white boots, Katie was staring at two hairy front hooves. How gross was that?

Wait a minute. Hooves? Katie didn't have hooves. They weren't something fourth-grade girls stood on. Fourth-grade girls had feet.

But *reindeer* had hooves. *Hairy* hooves. Just like the ones Katie was staring at right now. And that could only mean one thing.

The magic wind had switcherooed Katie into one of Mr. Frost's reindeer! Katie believed in getting into the Christmas spirit as much as anyone—but this was ridiculous!

Katie licked her hairy reindeer lips. Boy was she thirsty. And before she could stop herself, Katie suddenly lowered her head and antlers and began licking at the snow on the ground.

Hairy lips? What a yucky thought. Still, Nick was right. Her reindeer lips weren't chapped at all, despite the cold snow. That hair sure came in handy.

Suddenly, Katie felt someone petting the back of her neck. "Kids, this is Randy the reindeer," she heard Tom say. "He's leading our sleigh tonight."

Katie turned her head and gulped. A bunch of little kids were in the sleigh. And did Tom just say she was supposed to lead it? How did you do that? She had no idea where to go. Tom was making a big mistake.

But there was no way to warn Tom that Randy the reindeer wasn't up for the job. It wasn't like she could actually talk to him or anything. After all, Katie wasn't Katie right now. She was a reindeer. And Katie was pretty sure that even though Tom loved reindeer, he couldn't actually *speak* reindeer.

"Okay, is everybody all bundled up?" Tom said as he climbed onto his seat at the front of the sleigh.

"Yeah!" Katie heard the children shout.

"Then, giddyup!" Tom cheered.

And with that, they were off. Katie started walking slowly at first. It was hard getting used to the strange sensation of pulling a sleigh over slippery, icy ground.

Luckily, her hooves were like big, hairy snowshoes.

After a few minutes, Katie got the hang of it. Her hooves began to move faster and faster through the woods. The sleigh was heavy. However, with the other reindeer helping, it wasn't as hard to pull as she thought it would be. And it felt so good to be running, to feel the cold air rushing around her. Her hairy lips broke into a smile. Even though she was hooked up to a sleigh, she felt really free, and really happy.

And then, suddenly, she smelled something in the air. It wasn't a smell she recognized, but the smell frightened her. It wasn't anything she could put her finger (or her hoof!) on. She just sensed that something was wrong.

Arooooo!

Katie's reindeer ears perked up at a howling sound coming from behind. Her reindeer heart began to pound harder.

Arooooo!

A wolf! There was a wolf in the woods somewhere. And he sounded hungry. That wolf would probably like a yummy reindeer dinner right about now. Or maybe some juicy little children!

Katie gulped. Either way, this was nothing to "ho, ho, ho" about!

Chapter 18

Grunt! Grunt!

At first, Katie didn't even realize that the loud noises were coming from her throat. She didn't even know reindeer could make noises. But there she was, grunting a warning to the other reindeer behind her.

Grunt. Grunt. Grunt. "There's a wolf in the woods!" she called to the other reindeer

"What's the matter, Randy?" Tom asked.

Katie couldn't answer him. She could only grunt. So that's what she did.

Grunt, grunt. "We have to get out of here!"

Katie's hooves picked up speed. She was running as fast as her reindeer legs could carry her. But it wasn't fast enough. She could still hear that wolf.

Arooooo! He sounded like he was getting closer.

Katie had to get off the path. From the corner of her eye she spotted another path that forked off just to her left. If she could just make the turn fast enough, she could get out of the way of the oncoming wolf.

Quickly, she made a sharp left turn, dragging the whole sleigh with her down a cold, snowy path.

"Whoa!" Tom shouted. "Whoa, Randy. This isn't the right way."

But Katie wouldn't stop. She ran faster and faster.

"No, Randy! This road hasn't been plowed yet!" Tom shouted louder. He pulled on the reigns, trying to stop Katie and the other reindeer. But it was too late now. The other two reindeer had heard Katie's warning grunts. They knew that meant they had to run.

And run they did. For a minute, Katie's hooves were moving so quickly, she felt like she really was flying. Just like Dancer or Prancer or Rudolph!

Bam!

And then, suddenly, she stopped short. The sleigh behind her would not move, no matter how hard she and the other reindeer tried to pull. It was stuck.

"What's wrong?" one of the kids in the sleigh called up to Tom.

"We've hit a little snow bank, folks," Tom told the passengers. "Nothing to worry about."

"What do you mean *nothing to worry about*?" a girl said. "We're stuck out here in the cold, and we can't get out."

"I'm freezing," another girl said. She sounded like she was going to cry. "And it's getting awfully dark."

Tom flicked the reindeer reigns. "Come on, Randy," he said. "You and the other reindeer have to give it all you've got."

And that's what Katie did. She took a deep breath, and tried to pull the sleigh. The other reindeer pulled as hard as they could, too. Still, the sled didn't move an inch.

"We're really stuck," one of the kids said nervously.

Katie could sense that Tom was nervous now, too. It was getting colder and darker by the second. The children in the sleigh were upset. One sounded as though he was going to start crying.

Not that Katie blamed him. She would have cried too—if she could. But reindeer didn't cry. And Katie *was* a reindeer. A big, scared reindeer. A big, scared, STUCK reindeer.

Suddenly, Katie sensed something coming toward them. Was it the wolf again? No! The sound was different.

A moment later, a snowmobile appeared along the path. It stopped a few feet from the sleigh. A man got off and walked over toward the sleigh.

As the man came closer, Katie's hairy lips broke into a big smile. She knew that man. It was Mr. Frost. He'd driven the snow mobile out here to find the sleigh.

Hooray! They were saved.

"You've been gone so long, I figured I

better come looking for you," Mr. Frost said as he walked over to the sleigh. "How did you wind up on this path, Tom?"

"I don't know," Tom admitted. "Randy just took off all of a sudden. He must have been spooked by something."

Katie tried to nod her head. She wanted Tom to know he was right.

"That's never happened before," Mr. Frost told the passengers in the sleigh. "These reindeer have been here most of their lives. They know how safe it is here. The whole park is fenced in. Nothing can get in here to hurt them."

Katie frowned. She hadn't known that. She thought everyone might have been attacked by a wolf. She'd gotten everyone stuck in a snow bank for no reason at all. And now Tom could be in trouble. After all, he was responsible for controlling the reindeer and keeping the passengers safe and on the right path.

"I honestly don't know what happened,

Mr. Frost," Tom said, shaking his head. "One minute everything was fine, and the next minute Randy was taking us on a wild ride."

"Well, I'm just glad you're all safe," Mr. Frost said.

"Let's get you back where you belong," Mr. Frost said to the passengers. "Let me help you out of the sleigh. That will make it much lighter. Then Randy and the other reindeer will be able to pull it out of the bank."

One by one the passengers got out of the sleigh. Then Tom flicked the reigns. Once again, Katie and the other reindeer tugged at the sleigh. And this time, it moved!

"The sleigh's out of the snow bank," Tom called to Mr. Frost.

"Okay!" Mr. Frost replied happily. "Now let's load these kids into the sleigh and take them back to the gingerbread cottage. I think they're ready for some hot chocolate!"

"We sure are," one of the girls agreed.

"Keep the sleigh on the main path all the

way back," Mr. Frost said to Tom.

"I'll try," Tom assured him.

So will I, Katie thought to herself. *I'm not getting stuck again!*

Chapter 19

A little while later, the children were returned to their parents. The reindeer were unhitched from the sleigh and back in the barn. Everybody was where they were supposed to be.

Except Katie, of course. She was still Randy. And that wasn't the way things were supposed to be at all.

"Here you go, Randy," Mr. Frost said. "Have some nice mushrooms."

Katie happily nibbled the food from Mr. Frost's hand. She was glad reindeer were vegetarians, just like she was.

"What a night," Mr. Frost told Tom. "It's our busiest one yet."

"It was definitely not the best time for Randy to go on a joy ride," Tom agreed.

"When Christmas is over, I'm going on a long vacation," Mr. Frost said. "It's been so busy here, I haven't even gotten to decorate my own house. I'll bet my place is the only one in Cherrydale without lights or decorations."

"Now, that's a shame," Tom said.

Mr. Frost sighed. "Well, come on," he said. "We have more customers waiting for sleigh rides. At least I think we do. I hope the parents of those kids didn't scare people off by telling them what Randy did."

Katie frowned. She hadn't meant to cause Mr. Frost trouble. She was just running from a wolf.

"Having a runaway reindeer is bad for business," Mr. Frost continued. "I think Randy should stay here in the barn at least for tonight. Give him time to settle down."

Oh no! Katie thought. Poor Randy. He was getting the blame for something that had been Katie's fault.

"The other reindeer seem okay to go for another run," Tom told him. "I'll hitch them back up. We'll be ready in a few minutes."

With that, Tom and Mr. Frost left the barn. Now Katie was all by herself, chomping on the mushrooms Mr. Frost had left for her.

But Katie wasn't particularly hungry anymore. She felt bad for Mr. Frost. And she was also worried. It was dark out. Nick must be really upset that Katie was still missing.

Katie had sure caused enough trouble for one night.

Just then, Katie felt a cold breeze blowing on the back of her long, thick reindeer neck. She looked around the barn. The windows weren't open and the doors were shut tight. So where was that draft coming from?

It didn't take Katie long to figure that one out. Suddenly that cold breeze became a wild, blustery, icy wind. It was a wind that didn't have to come through doors or windows. This was the magic wind!

The magic wind grew stronger and stronger, blowing wildly around Katie. It whirled and swirled like an Arctic tornado. Katie shut her reindeer eyes tight, and tried not to cry.

And then it stopped. Just like that. The magic wind was gone.

Katie Carew was back. And so was Randy. He looked at Katie and let out a little grunt.

"Don't be afraid," Katie said, reaching up to pet Randy's furry head. "You're okay. And so am I." She frowned slightly. "Other than this terrible taste in my mouth. I ate too many of those mushrooms. I think I need a candy cane."

⭐ ⭐ ⭐

A few minutes later, Katie got exactly what she needed—a yummy, red and white peppermint candy cane. Nick was enjoying one as well. He seemed very happy—especially now that Katie was back where she belonged.

"You had me worried there, Katie," Nick told her as he added a few more marshmallows to his hot chocolate. "I had no idea where you'd gone. You should have told me you weren't going to try the maze."

"You're right. I'm sorry," Katie apologized.

There didn't seem to be anything else to say.

"The maze was so much fun, Katie," Jeremy piped in. "How come you didn't try it with us? Were you afraid you'd get lost or something?"

Katie sighed. She *had* been lost in a maze tonight. A maze of paths out near the woods. And that maze was blocked by snow banks, not metal candy canes. But of course she couldn't tell Nick or Jeremy about that. They wouldn't believe her even if she did. Katie wouldn't have believed it either if it hadn't happened to her.

Still, she had to say something. "I was walking around for a while, and then I was out at the barn petting a reindeer," Katie told Jeremy and Nick.

There. That was *kind of* like the truth, anyway.

"Leave it to you to want to spend your whole night with the reindeer," Emma W. said kindly. "You're the biggest animal lover I know."

"Okay, you guys," Nick said. "I think we should get going. Mr. Frost has a lot of evening customers coming now. They're going to want some hot chocolate, too."

"Is Mr. Frost going to be working all night?" Katie asked Nick.

"At least until midnight," Nick told her. "That's closing time."

Katie frowned. Midnight. That was really late. No wonder Mr. Frost hadn't found time to decorate his house.

She looked around. There was still a line of customers waiting to go on sleigh rides. "Look at all those people," she said. "I'm glad I didn't scare them away."

"You?" Nick asked. "Why would you scare them away?"

Oops. "I mean, I'm glad they're not scared to go on a sleigh ride in the dark," she said quickly.

"You didn't get to see Santa," Matthew said, interrupting Katie's conversation with Nick. "But I saw him. His workshop is right at the end of the candy cane maze. When I got there,

Santa was making toys with his elves! I got to sit on his lap and everything."

Katie smiled. She was glad Matthew had changed the subject.

"Do you want to see him?" Matthew asked her. "I could show you where he is."

"That's okay," Katie said. "Maybe another time."

"Santa's probably sleeping by now, anyway," Nick told Matthew. "He needs his rest. He's got a lot of work ahead of him."

"The reindeer have a lot of work ahead of them, too," Katie reminded Nick. "It's hard work pulling that sleigh." She rubbed her shoulder. "You have no idea how hard it is."

The kids all looked at her funny.

"I mean, we humans have no idea," Katie said quickly.

"Hey, do you guys know what reindeer have that no one else has?" George asked the kids.

"What?" Jeremy replied.

"Baby reindeer!" George exclaimed. He

started to laugh.

Everyone else laughed, too. Except Katie, that is. She was too busy watching Mr. Frost sell tickets to his guests. He looked so tired. As tired as Santa and his reindeer must feel on Christmas morning.

Chapter 20

"Deck the halls with boughs of holly," George and Emma W. began to sing.

"Shhh . . . we don't want to wake him," Katie whispered. It was early on Thursday morning. Katie and her friends had gone with her grandmother and Nick to deliver a special gift for someone they really liked.

"Mr. Frost was up really late last night." Katie hung some silver tinsel over a bush in his front yard.

"Won't Mr. Frost be surprised," Katie's grandmother told her.

"I can't wait until he wakes up and sees what we've done," Katie said. "He didn't have time to decorate his house himself."

"*We* barely have time to get it done," Emma W. said. "Christmas Eve is tonight."

"We'll get it done," Katie was sure of that. She looked around the front yard. George was hanging Christmas balls from the branches of a maple tree.

Emma W. and Jeremy were helping Nick string tiny, white lights on all the pine trees. Suzanne was hanging a paper wreath of cut-out handprints on the front door.

"This looks beautiful!" Katie exclaimed.

"It's a winter wonderland all right," Suzanne agreed. "And my wreath is the crowning touch."

Katie laughed. Suzanne never changed. And that was okay. Katie liked her the way she was. Usually.

"The wreath does look nice," she told her best friend. "I'm sorry you couldn't go with us yesterday."

"It's okay," Suzanne said. "I was busy at the Community Center selling candy again. I think

I must have broken a world record for selling peanut brittle."

"I'll bet you did," Katie told her.

"Okay, are we ready to get Mr. Frost out here?" Nick asked the kids.

"Oh yeah!" Katie and her friends shouted back.

"Then let's do it!" Katie's grandmother said.

The kids all ran up to Mr. Frost's front porch. They began to sing.

"We wish you a merry Christmas. We wish you a merry Christmas. We wish you a merry Christmas, and a happy New Year!"

Suddenly, the door opened. Mr. Frost stood there in his robe and slippers. He blinked a few times and looked out at the group of kids on his front porch.

"Isn't it a little early for carolers?" he asked them.

"We wanted to catch you at home," Katie told him. "You're always working in the afternoons and at night."

"That's true," Mr. Frost said with a smile. "This is a pleasant wake-up surprise."

"Oh, that's not the only surprise," Nick told him. "Take a look."

The kids moved out of the way to give Mr. Frost a better view of his front yard.

"Oh my!" Mr. Frost exclaimed. "This is so beautiful."

"Do you really like it?" Katie asked.

"I do," Mr. Frost told her. "In fact, this is the best Christmas surprise I've ever had. You know, in all the years I've owned the North Pole Winter Fun Park, I've never once been able to decorate my house."

"You don't have time to enjoy the holiday yourself," Katie said.

Mr. Frost nodded. "Taking care of a park is hard work. Those reindeer need a lot of care."

"But it's worth it," Katie told him. "They're really happy."

Everyone looked at her strangely.

"I mean, they seem so happy," she said to her

friends. "And the people who come to the North Pole Winter Fun Park are happy, too."

"Well, today, *I'm* the one who is happy," Mr. Frost told the kids. "Now why don't you all come inside? I'll make some hot chocolate. And I'll put a candy cane in every mug."

"All right!" George cheered.

As Katie's grandmother, Nick, Suzanne, Jeremy, George, and Emma W. headed into the house, Katie suddenly felt a cold breeze on the back of her neck.

Oh no, she thought nervously. *Not the magic wind. Not now.*

Katie stood there for a minute, her eyes shut. She was waiting for that tornado to start whirling and twirling around her. But it didn't. Instead, it just sort of stopped.

The breeze hadn't been the magic wind at all. It had been just an ordinary winter wind. *Phew.*

Katie was so happy not to be switcherooed again. She really didn't want to be anyone else today. She just wanted to be Katie Kazoo at Christmas.

Have a Very Crafty Christmas!

Rudolph the Red-Nosed Candy Cane

Katie loves giving homemade Christmas presents to her friends and family. This year, she's come up with a candy cane craft that looks like it flew straight from the North Pole!

You will need: a brown pipe cleaner; a candy cane; glue (or a hot glue gun and an adult to help you with it); a small, metal bell; a small, red pom-pom; a thin, green ribbon; small, wiggly eyes (these can be purchased at any craft store)

Here's what you do:

1. Hold the candy cane straight up and down, with the curved part facing down. The curved end of the candy cane will be the reindeer's face, and the straight part will be its body.

2. Place a brown pipe cleaner under the curved neck of the candy cane, and twist it into a V-shape. Bend each end of the shape into a zigzag shape to form Rudolph's antlers.

3. Glue the wiggly eyes to either side of Rudolph's face.

4. Glue the red pom-pom between the eyes. This is Rudolph's nose.

5. Place the bell onto a piece of ribbon. This is Rudolph's collar.

6. Tie the ribbon around the curve of the candy cane. Glue the collar to Rudolph's neck.

Once all the glue has dried, your Rudolph is ready to fly into a friend's hands. (Just be sure to explain that this candy cane reindeer cannot be eaten.)

George's Joke Book

This year, George gave each of his friends a handmade joke book for Christmas. He printed out jokes, and illustrated each one. Then he stapled the joke pages together into a book.

If you want to make a joke book for your friends, George is giving you a head start. Here are some of the jokes he used in his book. You can use them in your book, too!

What do elves learn in school?
The elf-abet

What did the Gingerbread Man put on his bed?
A cookie sheet

Which of Santa's reindeer has the cleanest antlers?
Comet

What has six legs, four ears, one tail, two rear ends, four eyes, two noses, and two mouths?

Santa on a reindeer

What do snowmen eat for breakfast?

Frosted Flakes

What did the sad ghost say to Santa?

I'll have a boo Christmas without you.

Which burns longer, a red candle or a green candle?

Neither. Candles burn shorter, not longer.

What do you get if you cross St. Nicholas with a detective?

Santa Clues

What do snowmen wear on their heads?

Ice caps

What do the elves sing on Santa's birthday?
Freeze a jolly good fellow . . . freeze a jolly good fellow . . . freeze a jolly good fellow, which nobody can deny.

Why are Christmas trees so bad at sewing?
Because they always drop their needles.

What's the difference between the Christmas alphabet and the regular alphabet?
The Christmas alphabet has no L (Noel).

What's the best thing to put in a Christmas pie?
Your teeth

Why do reindeer scratch themselves?
Because they're the only ones who know where they itch.

Where do snowmen and snow women like to dance?

At snowballs.

About the Author

Nancy Krulik is the author of more than 150 books for children and young adults, including three *New York Times* best sellers. She lives in New York City with her husband, composer Daniel Burwasser, their children, Amanda and Ian, and Pepper, a chocolate and white spaniel mix. When she's not busy writing the *Katie Kazoo, Switcheroo* series, Nancy loves swimming, reading, and going to the movies.

About the Illustrators

John & Wendy have illustrated all of the *Katie Kazoo* books, but when they're not busy drawing Katie and her friends, they like to paint, take photographs, travel, and play music in their rock 'n' roll band. They live and work in Brooklyn, New York.